This book belongs to

_____

A SCRATCH & SNIFF
HALLOWEEN

By Elizabeth Spurr

Illustrated by Maggie Swanson

STERLING

New York / London

STERLING and the distinctive Sterling logo are registered trademarks of
Sterling Publishing Co., Inc.

10 9 8 7 6 5 4 3 2 1

Published by Sterling Publishing Co., Inc.
387 Park Avenue South, New York, NY 10016
© 2009 by Elizabeth Spurr
Illustrations © 2009 by Maggie Swanson
Distributed in Canada by Sterling Publishing
C/o Canadian Manda Group, 165 Dufferin Street
Toronto, Ontario, Canada M6K 3H6
Distributed in the United Kingdom by GMC Distribution Services
Castle Place, 166 High Street, Lewes, East Sussex, England BN7 1XU
Distributed in Australia by Capricorn Link (Australia) Pty. Ltd.
P.O. Box 704, Windsor, NSW 2756, Australia

Printed in China

Sterling ISBN 978-1-4027-6067-9

For information about custom editions, special sales, premium and
corporate purchases, please contact Sterling Special Sales
Department at 800-805-5489 or specialsales@sterlingpublishing.com.

Harvest moonlight, beaming bright,
Wispy witches taking flight.

Toothy pumpkins, eyes alight.
Hooray! It's Halloween tonight!

Skeletons with rattling bones,
And gloomy ghosts make eerie moans.

Grinning goblins brew big trouble.
Gremlins rise up from the bubbles.

Murky monsters, making tracks,
Meet hissing cats with arching backs.

Ghastly bats, with wings a-beating,
Lots of children, trick-or-treating!

See what yummy treats they're eating!

Chewy, sticky popcorn balls.
Pass them out to one and all!

Jolly jumping jelly beans
In orange and black for Halloween.

Candy corn striped orange and white.
Can you resist these tasty bites?

Squishy, licorice-y spiders,

Steaming cups of apple cider.

Pumpkin pies with scrumptious spice.
"May we have a *bigger* slice?"

Taffy apple on a stick.
Many treats for many tricks.

Witches stuffed with fluffy sweets,
A giant feast on every street.

Ghosts are led around by mummies,
Who hold their hands and count their yummies.

While all the monsters on the scene
Shout, "BOO! Hooray for Halloween!"